Fritz, the Count of Agliè

by Fritz,

with Michele Dalcin Botts

Dedicated to:

Michael, Stella, and McKay, who continue to inspire through the ethers.

What began as a children's book soon evolved into something more. The following pages are a snapshot of Italy, specifically a small town called Agliè with a 12th century castle. Life there is described in colorful details by my feline friend and co-author Fritz, who when only weeks old, defied Fate and now resides in a villa.

Special Thanks Go To The Following

Fritz. My co-author and muse for inspiring me.

Sandra Werling for opening her home and her heart to me.

Laura DeRuyter for her imagination and her beautiful paintings.

Brad Upton for helping this book reach fruition.

John and Esther Good for introducing me to Sandra.

Jean Fogelberg for her encouragement and tips on self-publishing.

Frank Arbaugh for all his help and photoshop skills.

Carla and Kevin Gilmartin for giving me the digital camera that took these photographs.

Vanessa Grant for helping me grow and learn to enjoy serendipity.

DeeDee Gordon for her insights.

Charlie Oyama for his constant guidance.

Darryl Palagi for listening to all my re-writes.

My sweethearts, Brittney Salerno and Shelby Sparks for nurturing the "kid" in me.

Peter Kluge, my manager and friend, for always believing in me.

Buddy and LoLo for rescuing me.

Fritz, the Count of Agliè

My name is Fritz, and I am the Count of
Agliè… How's that for a bold opening
statement? NOT entirely true, but at the very
least I've captured your attention.

I should tell you that Agliè is pronounced ALL
YAY not agglee, and now that we've gotten that
out of the way, I shall begin. I am more
appropriately referred to as the "Goodwill
Ambassador" and not the Count. There actually
was a real Count of Agliè. His name was Filippo
di San Martino, but more about him later…

You might have guessed from the cover of this
little book that I am a CAT. Good!!! I must
admit I'm not always as regal as the portrait of
me on the cover of this book portrays me. In fact
it was a snapshot of me, in a very ungraceful
pose on the beautiful tapestry couch in the villa,

1

that gave Michele Botts the idea to write my story.

Michele was inspired to write my story for two reasons:

1. I am such a fascinating feline.
2. I hold much information on the town where I spend Spring and Summer each year, Agliè.

Most people, including Italians, don't seem to know where it is or anything about it. Agliè is in Italy. I might have forgotten to mention that. I feel it is my duty to inform all of you about this enchanting paese. (Pronounced pie-ay-zay, meaning a small town or village. f.y.i.)

Michele says I am a Character.

She is right!

She also says I am an old soul… Well, since cats have 9 lives I could have been here before, but I digress…

You would think from the portrait that I was born into royalty, but the real facts are far, far different.

Here goes… I was discovered by a kind Samaritan

by the side of the road in Torino, Italy. I was just weeks old, lying next to the body of my mother. The stranger who saved me was Claudia. She was driving by and noticed us in a ditch. Upon investigating further, she discovered it was too late for Mama, but not for me. She put me in her car and drove me to the vet's office. I had a broken leg and was in very bad shape. But I was a survivor. Once I was able to travel, Claudia transported me to her Aunt Sandra who adopted me.

That is how I came to spend seven months out of the year in Agliè... In a Villa no less!!!

I'm taken back to the city of Torino for the winter months where I live with my best friend and caregiver, Sandra Werling. I also share our flat with my brother Gipino, my sister Vicky, and my brother Kim. I know, I know, Kim's a girl's name, but Sandra liked it. So my younger brother is a boy named "Kim." (Don't forget she named me Fritz, and I'm Italian.)

Kim hates the city so he stays behind in Agliè full time. Every year Sandra would put him in the car with us for the winter trip to Torino, a 45 minute drive. After two days in our apartment

Kim would make her so miserable she would be forced to drive him back to Agliè.

So the elusive Kim gets the run of the Villa all to himself. Sandra has to hire a part-time caregiver for him, and of course checks in on him regularly because she is such an animal lover.

I suppose I should mention my cousins, the turtles. Perhaps they are tortoises. They're pretty big. There are six in all. Sandra has names for each of them, but I haven't learned to remember them. (It's not as if they come when you call them.) Sandra tells me they are omnivores, which means they can and DO eat everything. Besides the lettuce, tomatoes, figs, and other fruits from our garden, they eat the best Italian bread, pasta, and even prosciutto. They also hibernate, which means they sleep all winter. That is more sleeping than all of us felines combined.

Nice life!!!

Oh yeah, and they also can be a nuisance, especially when they try to climb (yep, really) the biggest tree in our yard. They only get so far up and then tip over backwards. I guess at that point you can say, "They depend upon the kindness of strangers" to put them right again. Anyway, Sandra likes them…

A cousin...

Here is something I bet you didn't know about our turtles. They are quite frisky in the romance department. Now, how can I put this delicately? They "date" a lot. Sandra is constantly separating them in the garden. If she didn't we'd probably have 16 instead of 6. More names to NOT remember.

All that dating, climbing trees, and eating, I suppose that's why they need to hibernate.

Actually, the real reason she has to keep an eye on them is that we have four males and two females. The ideal ratio should be one male to four or five females. All but the original two turtles were born at the villa and Sandra doesn't have the heart to give away the three extra males. Anyway I really don't understand it, but Sandra says it has something to do with the male's strong nails damaging the female's carapaces. (That's a fancy word for shell.) Too much information!!!

Photo by Vanessa Grant

Our home.

6

Sandra's enchanted garden.

You'll see I've included some pictures of our domain and the wonderful garden Sandra lovingly cares for. It is such a magical place that we get visitors, friends of Sandra's, from all over the world. That's how I met Michele Botts. The real reason for this book, besides sharing me and my family with you and yours, is to introduce you all to the town of Agliè. Michele found it quite curious that so many Italians had never heard of it. She would tell them it was just outside of Torino (The first capital of Italy, from 1861-1864.), but they would draw a blank. Once Michele stayed here, she felt it was time to share her find.

Michele told me that years ago she and her husband Michael would sail their boat "Cygnet" (that means young swan) to an island called Catalina. It is located 26 miles off the coast of California. They were surprised to find on their first trip to Avalon, the main center of the island, a statue of a cat. A cat named Leroy. Apparently he was famous. He lived to be 20 years old.

One day while they were browsing in a used bookstore, Michele came across a little book written by Leroy, with some help I'm assuming. That book was called *Leroy, The Catalina Cat*.

It was all about his friends and adventures, but it was mostly written to introduce the "mainlanders," as they are called, to his precious island. So naturally when Michele met me and was introduced to the town of Agliè, she thought we should write a book too! So began our collaboration.

Now I don't want to give you the idea that I think I deserve a statue of my likeness in the town center. That would be quite bold of me. From what I heard about Leroy, he really deserved his statue.

Michele read to me the part in the book where he was kidnapped from the island of Catalina by a yachtsman who had grown fond of him. Once the locals investigated, they discovered who took Leroy and tracked him down on the mainland. He was only gone for a week, but apparently Leroy was more than anxious to return to Catalina. He always said he didn't belong to anyone in particular and felt his captor had some nerve taking him. I think I would have liked this guy.

By the way, Leroy referred to himself as the King of Avalon. I think calling myself the Count of Agliè is pale in comparison. Oh well, I guess we are both legends in our own minds.

Here are some photos of our family. The lovely Sandra. Vicky my older sister. There is the baby Kim, who is more like a ghost usually appearing at mealtimes. Our brother Gipino, who sleeps more than I do. Then there's me, who you already know.

The lovely Sandra

Vicky in the vines.

Kim caught off guard.

Gipino reflecting

Me reposing.

I've also included pictures of the main attraction in Agliè, the Castle. Agliè is a small town in the hillsides of northern Italy. It is located in the region of Piedmont. Sandra is such an aficionado on the castle that she gives private tours there once a week.

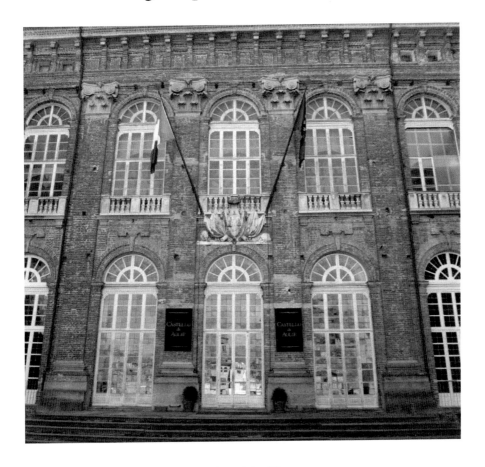

This is the entrance to the Castle of Agliè.

The back of the Castello di Agliè being photographed by
Michele's friend Vanessa.

A view of the garden from the castle windows.

Statuary on the castle grounds: A lion

A fountain.

Stone fruit.

One side of the castle.

Michele loves these windows.

Another view of the gardens with really tall statues.

A beautiful garden walkway leading to this sunlit interior.

20

Now that's what I call a hallway.

Nice lamp!

Hand painted birdies on the ceiling.

A few years back some cinema people decided to film a television series here in Agliè at the castle. It was called *Elisa di Rivombrosa*. Since it was a period piece set in the 1700's, the castle was made to look just like it did in the 18th century. I'm sure the castle walls were brimming with bygone spirits remembering the "good old days."

This reminds me of a story I heard concerning the woman who people say is the ghost of the Castle of Agliè. Her name was Vittoria di Soissons. She was born in the 17th century and according to history was a famous and frightful woman during her era. She was also quite willful. There is a rather scary looking wax bust of her in one of the salons in the castle. It is encased in glass. It is her from the neck up. (Not her best feature.)

The story goes that Princess Vittoria, who was never a beauty, not even close, married against the wishes of the court at age 52, an Austrian prince 20 years her junior. The marriage was a disaster. After living in Vienna for two years with her new husband, she fled back to Torino where she remained until she died at 80 years old. Since Vittoria married so late in life there was no chance for children, thus she left her entire inheritance to Benedetto Maria Maurizio, the Duke of Chiablese.

Me and Vittoria. (She's been airbrushed a little.)

It was this Duke who donated the bust of Vittoria as a sort of thanks for the inheritance he received. He could have airbrushed her a little I think. In life Vittoria never even visited the Castle of Agliè, but apparently the "ghost" of Vittoria entertains herself by playing pranks on unsuspecting visitors whenever it strikes her fancy.

I mentioned at the opening of this little book that there was a real Count of Agliè whose name was Filippo di San Martino of Agliè. Although very little is known about his entire life, he was a very important figure in the history of the castle. He lived in the 1600's and was responsible for turning the fortress of Agliè into a real castello. As Sandra began to tell me more about Count Filippo, I discovered he and I had a lot in common. For instance, he was apparently quite handsome (as am I), but he never married and consequently had no children. This was his choice. However in my case, I was forced to be neutered, thus making the possibility for my descendants impossible. Too bad!! I wasn't very happy about it at the time, but Sandra said it was the responsible thing to do.

The great love of Filippo's life was a duchess. Her name was Christina of France, Duchess of Savoy, and Queen of Cypress. My only introduction to courtship was a brief encounter with Cleo, a neighborhood stray. She is but a faint memory to me now, but I can still recall how she moved soft as a breeze, yet as startling as moonlight when she scaled the villa walls to be with me.

Count Filippo was a very interesting person in the history of Piedmont because he tried vehemently to protect its independence against France. That is why he was imprisoned by the famous (or should I say infamous) Cardinal Richelieu. You might recall Cardinal Richelieu from The Three Musketeers, if not Google him. Count Filippo was only released from prison in France after the Cardinal died.

For me to say I was ever imprisoned is an embellishment. However I was detained in a cat carrier just long enough to be delivered to the vet's office. This time I was kidnapped against my will and altered without my permission. I got over it.

After his release from prison, Filippo went back to Agliè and had his castle restored and enlarged by a famous architect. He turned his castle in to a real mansion of delights. Here they engaged in magnificent feasts, banquets, balls, and all sorts of amusements. Of course I was not able to witness all those wonders since my time was still to come, but Sandra has described them in vivid detail.

To tell the truth, I find it much more amusing to play with my siblings Gipino and Kim. Of course this does not require music and fancy dress. We are simple souls who enjoy ourselves in simple ways. Still, I assure you that we have a very good time. Sometimes we try to involve our sister Vicky in our games. However Vicky is a lady and disdains our rough manners. Still she is very sweet and we enjoy her company.

The official name of our castle is the Ducal Castle of Agliè. Something you might find interesting is that in the early 1800's Napoleon's army took over the castle after the French Revolution. His army pillaged all of the beautiful contents and left it in such terrible condition that the once majestic castle was turned into an alms house. Loosely translated, this means it became a home for the poor.

Sandra told me that at the restoration (when old monarchies went back to their thrones), the castle was returned to its ancient splendor with another king of the House of Savoy, Carlo Felice.

Fortunately, that is why today you can still visit and enjoy it.

I have included a chronology (that's a list) of dates and events significant to the Castello di Agliè. This will give you an idea just how far back in time it goes.

CHRONOLOGY

Between the 12th and 16th centuries the castle was the fortress for the San Martino dynasty at Agliè.

From 1642 thru 1657 the first transformation was ordered by Filippo di San Martino di Agliè and attributed to architect Amedeo di Castellamonte.

In 1764 the castle is acquired by Carlo Emamuele III for his second son, Benedetto Maria Maurizio, Duke of Chiablese.

Between 1766 and 1779 the second building transformation is ordered by the Duke of Chiablese and executed by Birago di Borgaro.

In 1771 Michel Bernard designs the garden.

During 1788 small projects were begun to reuse the interiors of the castle. This was performed by Domenico Marocco.

Between 1802 and 1814 there was the Napoleonic domination of the castle after which it was turned into an alms house.

In 1815 the castle is returned to Marianna, the widow of the Duke of Chiablese, who wills it to Carlo Felice in 1823. The castle passes into the Savoy dynasty.

In 1825 King Carlo Felice takes over the castle and commissions Michele Borda of Saluzzo to do the renovations.

The third transformation takes place between 1825 and 1830. Michele Borda supervises a qualified team of artists and craftsmen for the redecoration of the interiors.

In 1831 the castle passes to Maria Cristina, the widow of Carlo Felice, who orders the redecoration of the Royal Apartment.

The beginning of the newly landscaped park starts in 1839.

In 1849 the castle passes over to Ferdinando, Duke of Genoa, and becomes a simple retreat.

In 1856 the castle is inherited by Elisabetta of Saxony, widow of Ferdinando, who modifies the décor, mainly in the Green Gallery.

The exterior is completed in 1881. The roofs are evened out. The great flower bed in front of the castle is laid out.

Between 1883 and 1931 Tommaso, the second Duke of Genoa, continually modifies the castle's functionality and decoration.

In 1939 the state acquires the castle from the Duke of Genoa. In the 1960's the supervisor of monuments in Piedmont, Umberto Chierici, promotes substantial maintenance work on the castle and the redecoration of it's interior.

OUR HOME

I thought you might like a little history on the place I share with Sandra and our extended family in Agliè. I call it a villa. Sandra refers to it as a "casa." It was built around the middle or end of the 1800's. Sandra is not sure. Her grandfather decided to enlarge it at the beginning of 1930. It was called a "summer house," and so it remained until WWII. Her family resided there, especially in September, after having spent two months at the seaside before returning to Torino for the winter. Sandra's mother told her that many families gathered in Agliè in the late summer.

Many young people toured the countryside on their bicycles, attended dances, and truly enjoyed themselves at this time. That all changed when WWII broke out. All the families that could leave Turin (as it was called) left because it was considered very dangerous. The Germans were destroying factories, especially Fiat, and many homes were bombed and people were killed. Sandra's family, like many others, fled to the country where it was not as dangerous and remained there until the end of the war in 1945.

When Michele came to visit us for the first time, she noticed a framed document hanging inside our front porch. She asked what it meant and was intrigued to

find out it was issued by the Swiss Consulate.
Sandra's father was Swiss and Switzerland was
considered neutral. Essentially it stated that our villa
was protected and could not be intruded upon.
Sandra explained this document, which was issued in
1943, was not really of much use since the house
was occupied all the same. She believes it was taken
over twice by the Germans and also searched by the
Fascists. (Mussolini's followers.)

At the end of WWII the American Army came to Agliè, and not knowing where they could live, stayed in private homes and, of course, the castle of Agliè.

That document remains framed and fading in our front porch today. It's a reminder of how things used to be. When I think of the history of the Castello di Agliè, and the events that took place, I'm reminded that people don't always get along. I'm happy to say that here in our little oasis, Sandra and I, my siblings and the turtles co-exist peacefully and with joy. I believe we are setting a very good example.

Well, I'm ready for my nap now. So I'll close by inviting you to visit our historical "piccolo paese." You will definitely enjoy our fabulous scenery, great food and wine, and genuine hospitality.

I would also encourage everyone who reads this little collaboration to find it in their hearts to rescue a "friend" if the opportunity ever presents itself.

Who knows? You could just end up with a charming fellow like me.

Ciao, Fritz.

My Portrait by Laura DeRuyter.

The turtles painted by Laura.

EPILOGUE

Long before I met Fritz and fell under his charms, I had an ongoing love affair with cats beginning on my 28th birthday. I was gifted "Rudi" by my then boyfriend and future husband, Michael Botts. It was a beautiful Saturday afternoon in late September and Michael and I were running a simple errand. He parked the car and went into the dry cleaners to pick up his laundry. I waited in the car. Michael came out smiling and asked me if I ever had a cat growing up. I told him, "No." We were more like dog people. He pointed out a large cage of adorable kittens in the back of the cleaners. Their back wall was glass and faced the parking lot where we were parked. I hadn't even noticed. He announced he was going to introduce me to the wonderful world of felines. We should go back inside and I could take my pick. "Happy Birthday!" Thus began a lifetime of appreciation for these intuitive characters.

Michael and I had many cats over the course of our more than 25 years together. Some lived with us and some just visited. We always talked about writing a book about the cats we'd embraced and loved throughout the years. In fact, not terribly long ago I discovered an old envelope filled with pictures of the cats we'd complied. Some were ours, some belonged to friends and others were strays. Written on the outside of the envelope were the words, *Future Cat Book*. Unfortunately my husband Michael passed away before we could make that book a reality.

A few years ago one of my husband's close friends, John Good, invited my sister Carla and I over to his house to meet someone special. John and Esther Good had continued to include me in their lives even though Michael was now gone. The person they wanted us to meet was Sandra Werling. She had known John's father for over 40 years. They had met when John's family was living in Italy while his father was there working. Sandra was so elegant and beautiful. She told my sister and I about her home in Agliè, and extended an invitation for us to visit her there if we ever came back to Italy. I had no idea at the time what an integral part of my life she would become.

A few months before Carla and I met Sandra we made a trip to the Amalfi coast with some of Michael's ashes. My husband and I were sailors and always talked of going to Italy together, but never had.

I decided that Michael could still go with me in some form. I would leave a little of "him" behind in Ravello. The sea was staggeringly beautiful and the moon was full. I think he would have approved.

The following year I decided to go back to Italy, but this time I wanted to go to Florence to study Italian. When John Good found out I was going to Italy again he said, "You must visit Sandra at her villa." I told him I was sure Sandra was just being kind when she extended that invitation to stay with her in Agliè. John insisted Sandra would be hurt if she knew I was coming all the way to Italy and didn't look her up. With John's encouragement, I contacted Sandra and told her of my plans. She was delighted I was coming and gave me all the instructions I needed to get from Florence to Torino. She planned to pick me up at the train station and then drive less than an hour to the town of Agliè.

Sandra was so generous and gracious I felt as if I had known her for a long time. When I arrived at her "casa" the first cat to greet us was Gipino. The minute he heard the electronic gate rise up to allow the car to enter, he was there waiting like a sentry. I then caught a glimpse of Kim, but in a flash he was gone.

I took my luggage upstairs and entered the bedroom allocated for me. I glanced over towards my bed and noticed a handsome British short hair asleep on the bedspread. He opened his eyes and stared at me for the longest time. He didn't run off. He just stayed there fixated on me. I put down my bags and approached him. He allowed me to stroke his beautiful fur. Just then Sandra appeared and introduced me to Fritz. She then informed him he must leave so I could get settled in. I took an immediate liking to him.

Outside the shuttered windows I heard a rustling noise coming from the vines that dangled from the roof. I then met Vicky, the oldest of Sandra's rescues. She looked like a kitten even though she was well into her teens. I had now met everyone except the turtles.

Sandra's home was magnificent. It was like something out of a movie. The awnings were made of red and white striped fabric and the wicker patio furniture was painted in red lacquer. Oversized hydrangeas, my favorite flower, were abundant throughout the grounds. Her enchanted garden had a crimson lacquered bench. Perfect, I thought, for reflecting.

The red bench after an evening thunderstorm.

After my nap I headed downstairs for dinner with Sandra. There was a beautiful tapestry couch in the dining room where I once again caught sight of Fritz. He was grooming himself. I had my camera with me and caught him off guard when I snapped his photo. He again stared a hole in me. This time I was sure he was studying me. It was almost as if he knew I was broken. Did he hold some secret? He quickly jumped off the couch and approached me. He lay at my feet, rolling around, proposing I pet him, which I happily did. I felt an instant affinity for this cat who was a stranger to me just a few hours earlier. I have always felt that we get what we need when we need it.

Fritz was going to be my salvation. I just knew it.

During dinner Sandra explained to me how she came to adopt Fritz. What a story! That night as I was lying in my comfy Italian bed, I started going over all the events that lead me to be a guest in Sandra's beautiful home. How strange life could be was what I kept thinking. Even though Michael had never met Sandra, he was indirectly responsible for me meeting her. I knew I was here at this time in my life for a reason.

I started thinking about Fritz and the way he stared at me as though he was trying to burrow a way into my soul. I thought of Michael again and that cat book we'd always intended to write together. Was I led here to Agliè to complete something I didn't know I'd started? All I did know was since I lost my husband I was just going through the motions of living a life. I was working, traveling, and just trying to figure out who I was, separate from being a part of that coupling.

I was not really happy, but not exactly unhappy either. I was grateful for the 25 plus years Michael and I shared together, but at the same time, that's what made the future all the harder to face. Michael Botts had been my soul mate and mentor since we met when I was 22. We had a good life. I laughed everyday and woke each morning with a happy heart. When people would tell me I didn't look my age I would tell them, "Michael Botts gave me this face."

Genes also took some credit. My parents Stella and McKay gave me an awesome lineage. Now that my three cheerleaders were gone, the road to self-discovery seemed daunting. I participated willingly but with caution. By the time I met Fritz I was truly searching for something…

Something unexpected… Something telling.

Who would have guessed my adventure in Italy would culminate in this little book? It's been such a labor of love. So many friends came together, offering their time and talents, and all because I embraced the unknown. I let a wonderful cat, from a place I never heard of, come into my heart and heal me.

Thank you, Fritz!!!

The picture of Fritz that started it all.

AUTHOR'S NOTE

Shortly after writing *Fritz, the Count of Agliè*, I saw an interview with Blake Mycoskie on Tavis Smiley's show. I was familiar with Blake's face but not his back story. Blake is the founder of TOMS Shoes. In addition to being an entrepreneur he found a way to donate shoes, and now eyeglasses, to the many in need. I was inspired enough by Blake's interview to purchase his new book, *Start Something That Matters*. Now I am in no way an entrepreneur, but what I took from his book is that everyone does have a story to tell. That story matters. Big or small, we all have an opportunity to make a difference in this world.

I'm sure at one time or another we've all received unsolicited calendars or personalized address labels in the mail from a specific charity. Maybe not something we wanted or needed, but we still felt obligated to make a donation. When you buy a copy of *Fritz, the Count of Agliè*, hopefully you will enjoy the story. You should know you also made a donation to a worthy cause. All the profits from *Fritz* go to animal care and rescue. I personally benefitted from writing this little book because it helped me with the healing process I had been seeking. Knowing there is a chance my efforts can also aid in the comfort of animals makes me feel even better. Who knows, maybe Fritz and I actually did start something that matters. Thank you, Blake for your wonderful works and for sharing an important message.

We can all make a difference we just need to take the first step.

For more information on artist Laura DeRuyter go to
www.lauraderuyter.com

Additional information on Michael Botts can be viewed at
www.mikebotts.com

Made in the USA
Las Vegas, NV
26 January 2024

84909469R00033